The Gingerbread Boy

Adapted by Elizabeth Hastings from a popular 19th century folk
tale. Text © 1992 Random House Ltd. Illustrations © 1992 Liz
Tansley. All rights reserved. Random House Ltd, 20 Vauxhall
Bridge Road, London SW1V 2SA.
This edition published in 1992 by
Tiger Books International PLC, London
ISBN 1-85501-259-6
by arrangement with
Random House Children's Books
Printed in Hong Kong

The Gingerbread Boy

Retold by Elizabeth Hastings
Illustrated by Liz Tansley

TIGER BOOKS INTERNATIONAL
LONDON

Once upon a time there was a little old woman and a little old man, and they lived all alone in a little old house. They hadn't any little girls or any little boys, at all. So one day, the little old woman made a boy out of gingerbread; she made him a chocolate jacket, and she made him a bright little cap of orange sugar-candy. When the little old woman had rolled him out, and dressed him up, and pinched his gingerbread shoes into shape, she put him in a pan; then she put the pan in the oven and shut the door; and she thought, Now I shall have a little boy of my own.

When it was time for the Gingerbread Boy to be done, she opened the oven door and pulled out the pan. Out jumped the Gingerbread Boy and away he ran, out of the door and down the street!

The little old woman and the little old man ran after him as fast as they could, but he just laughed and shouted –

"Run! Run! as fast as you can!
You can't catch me,
I'm the Gingerbread Man!"

And they couldn't catch him.

The little Gingerbread Boy ran on and on, until he came to a cow, by the roadside.

"Stop, little Gingerbread Boy," said the cow, "I want to eat you."

The little Gingerbread Boy laughed, and said –

"I have run away from a little old woman,
A little old man,
And I can run away from you, I can!
Run! Run! as fast as you can!
You can't catch me,
I'm the Gingerbread Man!"

And the cow couldn't catch him.

The little Gingerbread Boy ran on and on and on, till he came to a horse in the pasture.

"Please stop, little Gingerbread Boy," said the horse, "you look very good to eat."

But the little Gingerbread Boy laughed out loud, "Oho! Oho!" and said –

"I have run away from a little old woman,
A little old man,
A cow,
And I can run away from you, I can!
Run! Run! as fast as you can!
You can't catch me,
I'm the Gingerbread Man!"

And the horse couldn't catch him.

By and by the little Gingerbread Boy came to a barn full of threshers. When the threshers smelled the Gingerbread Boy, they said, "Don't run so fast, little Gingerbread Boy, you look very good to eat."

But the little Gingerbread Boy ran harder than ever, and as he ran he cried out –

> "I have run away from a little old woman,
> A little old man,
> A cow,
> A horse,
> And I can run away from you, I can!
> Run! Run! as fast as you can!
> You can't catch me,
> I'm the Gingerbread Man!"

And the threshers couldn't catch him.

Then the little Gingerbread Boy ran faster than ever. He ran and ran until he came to a field full of mowers. When the mowers saw how fine he looked, they ran after him, calling out, "Wait a bit! Wait a bit, little Gingerbread Boy, we wish to eat you!"

But the little Gingerbread Boy laughed harder than ever, and ran like the wind. "Oho! Oho!" he said –

"I have run away from a little old woman,
A little old man,
A cow,
A horse,
A barn full of threshers,
And I can run away from you, I can!
Run! Run! as fast as you can!
You can't catch me,
I'm the Gingerbread Man!"

And the mowers couldn't catch him.

By this time the little Gingerbread Boy was so proud that he didn't think anybody could catch him. Then he saw a fox coming across a field. The fox looked at him and began to run. But the little Gingerbread Boy shouted across to him, "You can't catch me!" The fox began to run faster, and the little Gingerbread Boy ran faster, and as he ran he chuckled –

"I have run away from a little old woman,
A little old man,
A cow,
A horse,
A barn full of threshers,
A field full of mowers,
And I can run away from you, I can!
Run! Run! as fast as you can!
You can't catch me,
I'm the Gingerbread Man!"

"Why," said the fox, "I would not catch you if I could. I would not think of disturbing you."

Just then, the little Gingerbread Boy came to a river. He could not swim across, and he wanted to keep running away from the cow and the horse and the people.

"Jump on my tail, and I will take you across," said the fox.

So the little Gingerbread Boy jumped on the fox's tail, and the fox swam into the river. When he was a little way from the shore he turned his head and said, "You are too heavy on my tail, little Gingerbread Boy, jump on my back."

The little Gingerbread Boy jumped on his back.

A little farther out, the fox said, "I am afraid the water will cover you there; jump on my shoulder."

The little Gingerbread Boy jumped on his shoulder.

In the middle of the stream the fox said, "Oh, dear! little Gingerbread Boy, my shoulder is sinking; jump on my nose, and I can hold you out of the water."

So the little Gingerbread Boy jumped on his nose.

The minute the fox got on to the shore he threw back his head and gave a snap!

"Dear me!" said the little Gingerbread Boy, "I am a quarter gone!" The next minute he said, "My goodness gracious, I am three-quarters gone!"

And after that, the little Gingerbread Boy never said anything more at all.